CAMP KIDS

AND

THE TREASURE MAP

Stone Fence Publishing

JUMP HEADFIRST INTO MORE CAMP KIDS BOOKS...

BOOK 1
CAMP KIDS
AND
THE UNDERWATER ADVENTURE

...

BOOK 2
CAMP KIDS
AND
SERPY'S WILD ADVENTURE

CAMP KIDS

AND
THE TREASURE MAP

WRITTEN & ILLUSTRATED
BY SHARON SWAIN

PUBLISHER'S NOTE: This is a work of fiction. Although places in this book may be real, names, characters, and incidents are either the product of the author's imagination or are used fictitiously.

Cover design by Jonn Griffin and Sharon Swain

Published by:
Stone Fence Publishing
Burnt Hills, NY, 12027
USA

Printed in the United States of America
ISBN: 978-0-9827847-2-3
Copyright © 2011 by Stone Fence Publishing

www.stonefencepublishing.com

FOR MY MOM AND DAD

THANK YOU MARK, COLIN, GEORGETTE, KAREN, KRISTIN, DEBBIE,
DAMIAN, SUSAN, AND JONN

CONTENTS

CHARACTERS

Name: Grace Sophia Galley
Jobs: second grader, little sister to Cole
Interests: reading, writing, drawing, acting
Quote: "Hold on, let me just write that down."

Name: Colin (Cole) Mark Galley
Jobs: fourth grader, big brother to Grace
Interests: soccer, snowboarding
Quote: "Awesome. Yep, that about sums it up, awesome."

Name: Julia Anne Morgan
Jobs: second grader, stuffed animal collector, aspiring cook
Interests: anything new and hip
Quote: "Just write the company, tell them they're old news!"

Name: Jacob (Jake) Holden Leftwich, III
Jobs: fourth grader, quarterback
Interests: surfing, football, basketball, golf
Quote: "Dude, just watch me."

Name: Olivia Gabriella Finn
Jobs: fourth grader, big sister to Harvey
Interests: diving, swimming, water colors
Quote: "Well come on, let's check it out."

Name: Harvey Gabriel Finn
Jobs: third grader, little brother to Olivia
Interests: swimming and *Dr. Who*
Quote: "Just ask the animals, they'll know what to do."

Name: Leywa Hailey Casey
Jobs: year 5 student, older sister to Mali
Interests: bike riding, Motion Fresh
Quote: "Kevin is just so dreamy."

Name: Mali Aubrey Casey
Jobs: year 1 student, little sister to Leywa
Interests: adventure, monsters, dolls
Quote: "Let's go meet them."

Name: Caleb Toby Knudsen
Jobs: year 6 student, older brother to Lukas
Interests: skiing, kayaking, karate, pranks
Quote: "I've got this."

Name: Lukas Aiden Knudsen
Jobs: year 3 student, younger brother to Caleb
Interests: pranks, jokes, eels
Quote: "Let me say the punch line."

CAMP KIDS

AND
THE TREASURE MAP

CHAPTER 1
THE TREASURE MAP

"Dougal, give it back!" Cole yelled, chasing the small tan puppy with a red ball in its mouth.

Cole and his sister Grace were so excited when their mom and dad had given them the puppy. They were in the Adirondacks at their camp and their friends Julia and Jake had just come over to plan the last week of the summer when in walked the crazy, fluffy little puppy.

"Oh, just forget it," Grace suggested as the puppy dodged Cole again. "Come on, we can play catch later. I told Jake and Julia that we would meet them at the clubhouse to check out some new maps. Jake wants to try to ride the Rapids underwater." Grace knelt down to pet Dougal, who was now rolling around at her feet, the red ball abandoned at the edge of the mountain lake. "Yes, puppy, you can come too."

"Right on, sounds good. Come on boy, let's see who's faster," Cole called, taking off up the sandy path that led to the old abandoned cabin the kids use as a clubhouse. Dougal was right on his heels.

Eight-year-old Grace was always thinking, always planning, and *always* jotting down her ideas and sketches in her journal. She was already on her third journal for the summer. The first two were filled with the amazing adventures that she, Cole, Jake, and Julia had already had in their first month and a half at the lake. The small, appropriately named Pleasant Lake was where they all spent their summers in the Adirondacks.

The four kids had discovered something wonderful this summer: fairy stones. These glowing, magical stones had changed everything. With them, the kids are able to breathe underwater, travel through river channels to other lakes, and no matter how long they stay under or how far they travel in their new underwater world, time does not pass above water. A few weeks ago, with the help of Grace and Cole's cousins, the boys even saved a baby sea serpent.

In a car at the bottom of the lake, they had found a key with a wooden moose keychain. It was the moose key that opened the cabin they used as a clubhouse, and inside they had found books and maps and even a letter written to them. The letter told them that they were now water sprites and as water sprites they would need to use the magic of the stones to help protect the animals and waters of the world. The letter also mentioned that the magic of the stones would only last while they were young, but the kids decided not to worry about that yet. Needless to say, even before the arrival of Dougal, Grace had plenty to write about.

"Watch out, you crazy puppy," Cole laughed, tripping over Dougal. He rubbed the dog's fluffy head and carried on running up the path.

Grace watched as the dog continued to dodge in and out of Cole's legs, stopping now and then to sniff trees. She had to jog to keep up, giggling the whole way.

As soon as they arrived at the clubhouse, Dougal jumped straight into the outdoor fire pit. He began sniffing the edges of the circle of river stones.

"We're going to have to train this dog," Grace giggled, still watching Dougal who was now digging his nose through all of the ancient soot and charred sticks. "Get out of there, buddy, you're getting so dirty," Grace complained, walking over to the fire pit and trying to pull the puppy out. But Dougal was enjoying the great new game and kept jumping away from her. "Cole, help, he's not listening and I didn't bring any treats."

"I bet Julia has something. I'll go check," Cole offered, turning and running into the clubhouse, touching the wooden moose on the door as he went.

Jake and Julia were inside, chatting and eating cheese and crackers. Cole lifted Julia's chipmunk off the box of crackers, took one, and ran out of the cabin.

Chippy was Julia's animal guide. He was always at Julia's side, watching out for her, and enjoying the snacks that she always seemed to have on hand.

"Dude, what'd ya do that for?" Jake asked, turning to see Cole head out the door.

Jake, Julia, and Chippy all jumped up and followed Cole to the fire pit just in time to see Grace, black with soot, wrestling with Dougal. She was trying to get something out of his mouth.

"Dougal, look what I've got," Cole sang, holding out the cracker, hoping that the dog would drop whatever was in his mouth and take the food instead. But Dougal just looked up with his cute little eyes, trying to sniff at the cracker while still holding on tight to the item in his mouth. "What is that, anyway?" Cole asked.

"It's some kind of metal box, like an old pencil box or something," Grace grunted, struggling to tug at her end.

Jake, Julia, and Chippy giggled from the sidelines.

Dougal's ears perked up, he dropped the box, and swung around to see where the giggling was coming from. Then he saw Chippy. He pounced out of the pit and landed on the ground in front of the surprised chipmunk. The three kids froze, watching to see what would happen next.

Dougal sneezed, burped, and laid his head on Chippy's feet, looking up at him through his long hair.

Chippy, who was as surprised as everyone, leaned over hesitantly to pet the dog. Dougal nuzzled his head farther into Chippy's lap, accidentally knocking him over.

Grace looked at the old metal box in her hand. "Silly dog, what's so great about this?" She opened the

box and inside there was an old, faded piece of paper. "Hey you guys, check this out," she said, holding up the paper for the other kids to see.

"What is it?" Julia asked, pushing her glasses farther up her little nose.

"Let me see it," Cole said, reaching out to take the brittle piece of paper. He carefully started to unfold it.

"I bet it's a love letter," Jake teased. "Hey Cole, maybe it's from Olivia. Wouldn't that be nice?"

"No, look, I think it's a map. Look at those lines and there's an X," Grace said, taking back the map, and pointing to the faint lines that were only just visible on the paper.

"It's a treasure map," Cole said, rubbing his hands together. "I bet it'll lead us to gold."

"Or jewels," Julia dreamed, her eyes lighting up as she pictured herself wearing diamond-studded crowns, rings, and necklaces.

"Well, I guess we'll never know. There's no label and this whole corner is gone. The only thing we can read is this K and a scratched off P, up here at the top." Grace carefully folded the paper and put it back in the metal case.

"That stinks, I was thinking I could buy that undersurf board from the Surf's Down shop in Lake Champlain," Jake grumbled, reaching for the rusty old pencil box, just in case. He'd need to get a better look at that map before giving up completely. He might see something Grace didn't. After all, his dad is a part time treasure hunter. "Are we sure we can trust you with that?" he asked, pulling the case from Grace's hand.

"Don't be ridiculous, Jake," Julia said, grabbing hold of the box. "I'll take it. I mean I have my bag with me all the time and then we'll have it if we need it," she added with a smile, trying to pull the box away from Jake.

"But if you ever want to find the treasure I would leave it with Grace," Cole said, reaching for the metal box and watching his sister. "Look at her. She's already got a plan."

The kids watched as Grace packed map after map from the clubhouse table into her bag.

"I bet by tomorrow she knows where to look for the treasure," Cole said, taking the box from Jake and Julia and tossing it into his sister's bag.

"Whatever, I want to go swimming anyway. It's getting hot. We can check out the maps for Rapids at Otter Creek later. Meet you at the lake!" Jake yelled, running off toward his camp and adding, "See ya there, slow pokes!"

Dougal jumped up and took off after Jake. Cole ran after him trying to catch up.

Grace collected more maps and an old sprite journal from the shelf while Julia continued to talk about the treasures they might find if they could just figure out how to read that map.

CHAPTER 2
1, 2, 3 4

"So, I'm pretty sure I've figured it out. I checked all of the maps last night, and I think I know which lakes and rivers these are," Grace said, taking five maps out of her bag, opening them and carefully spreading them out across the clubhouse table. "There, you see?" she announced, looking up with a proud smile.

The other kids just stared at her waiting to hear an explanation, clearly they did *not* see. Dougal sat at her side, looking up at her, with his pink tongue just peeking through his furry lips. Chippy sat next to Dougal nibbling on a mini donut, his big eyes expectantly watching Grace.

"The treasure map; I know which lakes and rivers they are," Grace explained again, opening the old pencil box and carefully unfolding the brittle, yellowed piece of paper. She took a deep breath and carefully set the treasure map on top of the other maps on the table. "There. Now you see it, right?"

The kids all looked at the maps and looked back up at Grace again, obviously needing more explanation.

With another deep breath she dramatically slid a small torn piece of paper into place on the map. She looked up with a satisfied sigh and smiled, "That was still in the box. Look, it's the rest of the words, *KP-Motion Fresh 1,2,34.*"

The kids and animals stared at the map yet again. Julia even got up to look from another angle.

"Um, Grace, I'm sorry, but that really doesn't help," Julia said, squinting at the maps on the table. "It's the same as yesterday, but now I'm more confused. I mean, what's Motion Fresh? And why is the P crossed off?"

"And why did they forget to put the comma between the three and the four? Now that's just bad grammar," Cole joked. "It was probably just some punk who hid half of his sister's birthday cake or something."

Jake agreed, "I mean, come on, if you're going to make a treasure map at least you could say what the treasure is."

"Never mind that!" Grace snapped, taking another deep breath. "See, if you look at all of these maps, you can see that the shapes of the lakes and rivers match up," she said, pointing to the treasure map and lifting it to see the map below. "See, this is our lake and here is Otter Creek, and Moose River is right there; that must be Brantingham Lake, Lily Pond, and Lake of the Pines. But they all look different because this is a map of underwater, not land." Grace looked up and beamed at her friends. "As soon as I figured that out, it was easy. Those are the Chain Lakes and I think that one is Lake Champlain.

"The X is either somewhere here in the woods or in Lake Champlain. I'm not sure because whoever made this map made the river channels really short to save space and then turned things around too. And if you look really closely, you can see numbers too. There's a 1 right here in Otter Creek, near where the rapids are, and a 2 on one of the islands in Brantingham, and an X here in the middle. It might be at the golf course, or in the middle of Lake Champlain. I can't really tell."

"Well, where's the 3 and the 4?" Jake asked.

"Who made it?" Cole whispered quietly, thinking of all the time it must have taken to make the map. "Punk or not, whoever made it must've really wanted to hide the treasure. I take back my cake comment."

"I don't know all the answers, but I think we could work together to find out. I think if we start looking for number 1, we might just find our way to the X. What do you say?" Grace asked, putting her hand out.

"Hey, if there's treasure on the line, I'm in," Cole said, placing his hand on top of his sister's. "I mean, I do like cake so either way I'm good," he added, chuckling.

"Maybe there'll be pirates!" Jake cackled, adding his hand to the pile.

"As long as you promise to never leave me," Julia whined, slowly raising her hand and placing it on top of Jake's.

Grace smiled, "Right, one, two, three."

All of the kids shouted, "WATER SPRITES!"

"Awesome, that means we're headed for Otter Creek. I get to check out the Rapids after all!" Jake put both hands out pretending to be surfing; with his tan and Hawaiian-print swim shorts, he really looked the part.

Jake actually was a surfer, back home in California. But he spent all of his summers here in the Adirondacks with his grandparents and he missed the surf competition every year. He'd been surfing since he was three and he just found out that this year he qualified to compete in the teen division even though he was only ten. He had begged his dad to let him come home early so he could go to the competition, but like every other year the answer was no.

"Oh yeah, man, it's gonna be so great," Cole sang, joining Jake, putting his arms out and shifting his weight from side to side pretending he was riding a big wave. Cole had the shaggy blond hair, clear blue eyes, and floral print shorts of a surfer, but his bright white skin gave away that he was a true upstate New Yorker.

"Well, there's just one problem. I can't figure out how to swim to Otter Creek except through the creek itself and it's too strong and rocky," Grace said. "We're going to have to find a ride."

"Hey, my aunt Maryanne was just talking about bringing my cousins there," Julia said with a proud smile. "We could go with them."

"Great idea, but there's Johnny, Fraiser, and Andrew, plus the dog, and your uncle. And if you're invited won't your mom and dad want to go?" Jake asked. "There's no way we'll all fit."

Cole had been thinking the same thing, and he knew Jake's grandparents wouldn't want to go. "Well Grace, I guess that leaves us. I bet Mom and Dad would go, they love that place. And Julia, it will be perfect if your cousins are there. They can distract the adults while we look for the clue."

Julia's aunt, uncle, and her mom had retired fairy stones in the clubhouse. And even though they don't remember being water sprites, they still love the water. As a matter of fact all of their jobs are saving and protecting the water and animals. Julia's aunt makes documentaries about Clean Water Projects in Africa, her uncle is some sort of engineer in charge of approving environmentally responsible bridges and dams, and her mom volunteers at the Boston Aquarium, helping injured water animals return to their natural environments.

"Yeah, Mom and Dad are always trying to get us to go do that sort of thing," Grace agreed. "Julia, find out what time you're leaving and we'll make sure we go at the same time. Jake, you can ride with us. And yes, Dougal, you can come too." Dougal and Chippy had settled in for a little nap on the floor at Cole's feet, but as soon as he had heard his name, Dougal's ears perked up and he was waiting at Grace's feet.

*****

The four camp kids arrived ready for the treasure hunt. Julia packed the food and Grace updated her waterproof journal with all of the information that they would need about Otter Creek. Jake offered to look after the treasure map in the waterproof bag his dad had given him.

When they arrived at the end of the dirt logging road, Grace, Cole, and Jake began piling out of the Galleys' car while Julia and her cousins filed one by one out of the Morgans' minivan. Dougal scrambled over Jake's legs and jumped out, taking off up the trail after a chipmunk. The chip-munk was wearing a pair of sunglasses.

"Julia, what was that you just let out of your bag?" Johnny demanded as they stepped out of the van. "Your bag was moving and making noises the whole ride."

"No it wasn't, Johnny," Julia denied. "Now just stop being silly. I don't have anything in my bag, except," Julia dug deep into the backpack and triumphantly pulled out a candy packet, "these sour gummies. Want one?"

"Oh that's good, that's very good. You must have learned that one from the master," Johnny proclaimed, standing taller and rubbing his chest. "Yes, distraction by candy. I must say that is one of my classics." He reached out and grabbed the candy. "But you can't fool the master. I know you're hiding something." Johnny squinted and lifted two fingers to his eyes and then pointed at Julia and added, "I've got my eye on you." Then for good measure he turned to Grace, Cole, and Jake and did the same to them. "And that goes for you too. You're all looking a bit guilty and that's my job, not yours."

Johnny was the youngest of Julia's teenaged cousins, and today they needed Johnny to *not* pay attention to them. They needed him to distract the parents so that they could travel through the creek underwater without everyone freaking out.

"Hey Johnny, I bet I beat you down the rapids," Jake challenged, trying to distract him.

"You wouldn't have a chance, boy. I've been riding these rapids for years. But, today's not the day to show you. My dad is taking us upstream to try out fly fishing so you're on your own at the rapids." Johnny tipped an imaginary hat, "Ta, ta and remember, I make the trouble, not you." He turned and ran off up the trail.

"Well, I guess that gets a few people out of the way. Come on. Let's see who's staying with us," Cole said, turning and heading down the trail.

CHAPTER 3
OTTER CREEK

At the end of the trail, there was a massive rock, bigger than their whole camp. They climbed up it, higher and higher until it flattened out at the top where the river ran over the edge. The water level was much higher than in other years and the dark water was bouncing down over the rocks creating a natural turbulent water slide, otherwise known as the Rapids. It leveled out about fifty yards farther along into a fast running, wide creek.

There were two kids floating in the water on the top of the rock, slowly drifting with the creek as the current suddenly pushed them over the edge and into the rapids. They bumped up and down over the smoothed rocks. They were pushed here and there, under and over all the way to the bottom, where they had to swim with all their effort to make it back to the side before getting swept along with the current to the next, rougher set of rapids.

"Oh, baby, look how fast it is. This is going to be great!" Cole cheered, rubbing his hands together.

Jake marched straight to the top of the rapids, tying the string of his shorts tighter as he walked. He called back over his shoulder, "All right girls, you

check here around the rocks and trails for the first clue and Cole and I will head down the rapids and see if the clue is underwater." Jake could hardly contain his excitement. He was already sliding into the current, not waiting for a response.

"That's a good idea, right, Grace?" Julia asked. She had never actually gone down the rapids before. She had always managed to forget her bathing suit or hurt her ankle. One time she claimed that she had seen sea urchins in the water so she refused to go in.

The kids didn't have to worry, it was just Cole and Grace's mom who was staying with them, and she was just settling down on the rocks with her drawing pad. Everyone else had gone along the trail to find a good fishing spot.

"Mom, is it okay if we walk around a little bit?" Grace asked. "We're looking for something."

"Sure sweetheart, just take the walkie-talkie," Mrs. Galley answered, looking into her bag and pulling out a set of walkie-talkies. She handed one to Grace and rested the other on the rock beside her drawing pad. "What are you looking for?"

"We don't really know what we're looking for. We think there might be a clue around here somewhere. Here," she said, handing her mom her journal with the redrawn treasure map, "We found this. Dougal dug it up."

Grace's mom took the journal and gasped. "That looks like one of your Uncle Kevin's. He loved making treasure maps." She leaned forward to take a closer look. "Did it really say that?" Mrs. Galley asked, pointing to the words *Motion Fresh* on the map.

"Yeah. Why, what's it mean?"

Mrs. Galley laughed, "Oh, I don't remember, but I know I've heard it before. Did you know your uncle wanted to be a famous break dancer? He and his friend Pierre were planning on going to a national competition. They spent their whole summer one year selling golf balls and dancing."

Grace laughed, trying to imagine her uncle break dancing. "Did they ever make it?"

"Well, no. Now that you mention it, I don't know what happened. At the end of that summer, they just forgot all about the dancing and we all swam together every day." Mrs. Galley smiled and stared off toward the water. "That was a great summer. We spent all of our time in the water."

Grace was still trying to picture her uncle being a break dancer; the image just made her smile. Julia nudged her, trying to get her back on track.

Grace reached over her mom's shoulder and pointed to the number 1. "So, we're thinking that the 1 must mean that there's a clue around here somewhere."

Mrs. Galley continued to look at the girls, eyeing their fairy stone pouches, trying to make a decision. "Well, when I was a girl, actually I think it was at the end of that same summer," she hesitated, looking at the boys again, who were now walking up the rocks, each holding onto their fairy stone pouches, "I noticed there were some drawings on the rock at the bottom of the rapids, but it is very difficult to get to it. It's down deep. You would have to hold your breath for a long time. As a matter of fact, I don't know how I did it. The water must have been low that summer."

Mrs. Galley was lost in her own thoughts, remembering some of what she did and learned underwater, but not actually remembering being a water sprite. "Sometimes my memory isn't so good. But, I think it was right at the bottom of the rapids, where the water is very deep." She looked at the girls, smiled and picked up her paintbrush. "Good luck. I was always able to do whatever I wanted at your age. I bet you can too."

"Thanks, Mom, we'll check it out," Grace said, watching her mother and wondering what it will be like not to be able to use the magic of the fairy stone anymore and not to properly remember it either. "Hey Mom, how old were you that summer?"

"I guess I was about your age. Yes, I was eight. I remember because that is also when I started painting. That was the first of a few amazing summers," Mrs. Galley said, opening her paints and making a brush stroke.

Julia and Grace called to the boys and filled them in on the news from Mrs. Galley. Together the kids sat in a line at the top of the rapids, with the sunlight glistening off their skin. They let the current push them over the edge and into the rapids, disappearing at the bottom under the water. Dougal and Chippy, who had been playing in the water at the base of the rapids, stopped and waited for the kids to reappear.

"Where are Loony and Coolcat? I figured they'd be here by now," Cole asked, struggling to dive deeper into the very dark water. Loony the loon is Cole's sprite animal guide. And Coolcat is Jake's catfish guide.

"I was wondering that too," Grace replied. "It's so dark down here. Where does it end?"

"I don't think I like this. It's never dark when we dive," Julia moaned, grabbing hold of Jake's arm.

"Oh no, here we go again. Don't leave claw marks this time," Jake demanded. Julia had used him as a security blanket before. "Come on, Julia. Let's take a closer look at the rock surface. Maybe if we're closer we will be able to see it with our light."

Jake and Julia followed closer to the bedrock that had been eaten away by the waterfall over thousands of years, creating the very deep pool. The water was constantly pushing at the kids from every direction. Bubbles trapped in the tumbling water continuously floated past them toward the surface. It was like swimming underwater in a very dark, very bubbly, and very cold hot tub.

"This waterfall must have been a lot bigger once. I don't think this creek could have eaten away at this much of the rock," Grace thought out loud, wishing that she had purchased that underwater GPS at Sacandaga's Underwater Gear shop before it had closed for the season.

The kids were actually happy when they found out that the Sacandaga sprite town was only a traveling festival. The merpeople set up on June 28 each year and packed up and left without a trace on July 8. Since the kids didn't have enough money to buy any of the cool stuff, they just found it too frustrating to even be there. Of course Jake had found another Surf's Down shop in Lake Champlain and he begged the kids to travel there a few times so he could check out the undersurf boards.

"No kidding, that Light in All Darkness flashlight that we laughed at would be great right now," Cole said, holding his fairy stone pouch in front of his eyes, trying to use its light to see better.

Just then the kids felt the current change, and they saw a small light in the great darkness ahead of them.

"Hey, look at that!" Cole yelled, swimming faster toward the light.

"Cole, be careful, I'm not sure if it's safe," Grace worried, trying to catch up with her brother, who was now nearly at the light. Grace desperately tried to stay close but Cole just disappeared and so did the light. He was gone, just like that, and so were Jake and Julia. Grace was surrounded by complete blackness.

She looked back. She couldn't see Jake and Julia anymore, but she could hear Julia screaming and Jake complaining behind her. She looked back to where the pinprick of light had been. Jake would have to take care of Julia. Grace was going to find her brother.

A sheet of black spread out in front of her. Grace had nothing to guide her, except Julia's scream. Her own skin didn't even seem to glow at this depth. Where had Cole gone?

Grace was about to turn back and wait for Jake and Julia when the small light appeared again. It was right in front of her. She reached out and felt the bedrock. The light that started as a pinprick grew into a plate-sized circle. Grace slid her hand toward the circle and it passed through the rock. She reached her arm through the light and something grabbed her and pulled. She was wrapped in the light. It was hugging her and warming her like a blanket as her whole body was pulled though the hole in the rock.

CHAPTER 4
THE UNDERWATER DOME

The light was a door that opened into a cave, a bright beautiful cave full of incredible wall carvings.

Cole let go of his sister's arm. "Isn't it amazing?" he asked, looking around at the cave walls.

The wall behind Grace opened again and Jake and Julia tumbled into the cave. The light entrance closed behind them.

"Whoa, what's this place?" Jake asked, pulling each of Julia's fingers loose from his wrist while looking around the room.

Cole jumped as Loony and Coolcat suddenly appeared from behind them. "Hey, we were wondering where you guys were. Where did you come from? Did you find the clue?"

The loon and catfish swam around the cave shaking their heads back and forth.

"Wow," Grace breathed, looking at the cave's light grey, stone walls. It was a perfect dome, like a stone igloo. The floor was hard-packed dirt with a few perfect chair-sized rocks in a circle. The drawings on the cave walls were more like drawings in a child's sketch book than traditional cave wall drawings. They were probably made by water sprites, kids just like her. "The 1 must be there somewhere."

Cole, Jake, and Julia were already inspecting the drawings. After being pried off Jake, Julia took a deep breath, held her mother's necklace and closed her eyes for a few seconds. She and her mom had been working on a new calming technique, and it seemed to be working. She opened her eyes again and looked as calm as if she had just woken up. "Wow, these are great! I bet my mom made one of these, and your's too, Grace."

"Hey, check it out, this guy is surfing," Jake called, stopping to study the drawing in hopes of getting some new ideas.

Loony stopped swimming and was flapping his fins at part of the cave wall.

"What is it?" Cole asked, helping Loony to wipe the silt from the drawing on the wall. It was a number 1 with a picture of a dog digging into the ground where an X marked the spot. It was signed K-P-MF. "Hey you guys check out what I... I mean Loony found." Cole gave Loony a pat. "This is definitely it. Look, it's even signed." Cole pointed to the letters.

Grace had her journal out and was furiously writing. Julia was petting and praising Loony for a job well done, and Jake was already on hands and knees looking around on the floor.

"Here it is!" Jake yelled. "Here's the X." Jake cleared the thin layer of sand that sat on top of the bedrock and revealed a picture of a wobbly oval with a tree in the middle and a chain disappearing under it, into what looked like a hole or tunnel.

Cole rubbed his hands together. He knew what the clue meant. He was sure of it. Grace was quickly copying the picture into the notebook and Jake and Julia were both smiling ear to ear.

"I got it!" They all shouted together.

Julia was the first to finish. "It's that island in Brantingham where I got sucked into the Chain Lakes river channel."

"Dudette, like that's what I was gonna say," Jake complained.

"Well, I guess I know where we're going tomorrow," Cole said. "I wonder who K and P are anyway, and what the heck is Motion Fresh?" Cole asked, giving his friends a funny look.

"Who cares, as long as it's a good treasure?" Jake responded. "Come on let's get out of here. Did you guys feel how awesome it is to swim upstream under the water? I felt like I was a salmon or an otter or something. The water pushing against my face was wicked. Now let me just look at that drawing again. I've got to figure out how to surf these undercurrents."

Grace looked up from the journal. "Oh yeah, I forgot to tell you, Mom said she thought she'd heard of Motion Fresh before. She actually laughed when she read the name but she couldn't remember how she knew it. Then she started talking about Uncle Kevin and how he used to," Grace laughed again, "he used to break dance."

"Uncle Kevin, break dancing? No way. I can't picture that," Cole laughed, attempting to moonwalk across the dusty floor.

Jake joined in, diving to the ground and doing the caterpillar.

"Yeah, and Jake, you can be like his friend Pierre. Mrs. Galley said they were going to make it to a national competition," Julia giggled.

"K-Kevin, P-Pierre, MF-Motion Fresh," Jake thought out loud. "You've got to be kidding. Are you telling me that we're hunting for some break dancing moves book or something?" Jake grumbled. "I'm sorry, but that's not exactly a treasure is it?"

Grace thought about mentioning the money they saved for the competition, but Jake was just being so annoying. Who cares what Uncle Kevin left them, it's just fun looking.

"Whatever, punk, I'm just happy we found the first clue, ,cause you never know!" Cole punched Jake in the arm. "My uncle is cool. Even if it is a break dancing book, I could use some new moves." Cole flipped up on his head and attempted to spin, dust went flying in his eyes and mouth. He coughed and fell over laughing.

Jake watched, eyebrows raised, hands on hips, "Yeah, I'd say you could use some new moves. Come on, let's ride those undercurrents again." He headed toward the light and disappeared through the wall.

CHAPTER 5
DARK ISLAND

"My goodness, it seems early for the phone to be ringing," Mrs. Galley said as she stood up from her coffee and looked at the clock. "Eight-thirty, who could be calling at eight-thirty?"

She picked up the phone. "Hello... How are you, Olivia?... You would like them to come at 9:00?... If you're sure that you've already spoken with Jake's grandmother and Julia's mom, Mr. Galley and I will ride over with them at 9:00.... Yes, okay dear, we'll see you then. The kids will be so happy... Goodbye," Mrs. Galley said, hanging up the phone.

Harvey and Olivia were sprites too. They had a camp on the next lake over. The kids had all met at the car on the bottom of the lake earlier in the summer. The girls had also officially met Olivia at tennis lessons, so they were now land friends as well as sprite friends. Since they needed a good reason for being gone for so long to search the island, Cole left them a note in the glove box of the car asking to be invited over. So, the phone call was really no surprise.

Cole poured himself a bowl of cereal and found himself thinking of Olivia again. He was excited to see her. Jake had decided that Cole must be in love because his cheeks turn red every time he sees her. But Cole knew that was not it. Yes, she is beautiful but really it's just that she's so nice and calm and she seems to know everything about the underwater world. It's weird, he felt like he had always known her, even though they had only just met two months ago.

"Cole," Grace sang, waving her hands in front of his face. "Yoo hoo, snap out of it. Mom and Dad are ready. It's almost nine."

"Yeah, yeah. I'm coming," he snapped, hopping up from the table.

Jake was waiting on his bike outside his camp.

Julia, on the other hand, was not thrilled about the bike idea. She came out of her camp wearing her bike helmet, her prescription goggles, jeans (with extra stuffing for her butt), a long-sleeved shirt (even though it was already hot), knee pads, elbow pads, and something that was making her lips really puffy.

"Hi guyths," she greeted them, smiling and revealing fake waxed teeth.

"What on earth are you wearing those for? Aren't they supposed to be for Halloween?" Jake asked, trying to hold in his laugh. She looked so silly.

Julia slipped the fake teeth out of her mouth while she climbed up on her bike. "These are to protect my teeth if I fall."

She placed the teeth back in her mouth and began her deep breathing routine; eyes closed, deep breath in through flared nostrils, short puffs out through waxed teeth, repeat.

"Okay kids, let's make a move," Mr. Galley said, giving Julia a funny look. "Are you sure you're going to be all right?"

Julia opened her eyes. "I'm fine, thank you." She closed her eyes again and took one more deep breath.

Mr. Galley smiled and hopped on his bike taking the lead. Jake, Cole, and Grace quickly began pedaling. Mrs. Galley waited as Julia tried to get rolling. After falling three times, Mrs. Galley quietly steadied her and gave her a push and followed at the back of the line. She was sure that something was peeking out of Julia's backpack, but every time she thought she might get a good look, it disappeared.

*****

"We told our parents that we were going to row to the island," Olivia said, smiling at her friends. "They even packed us a lunch. But they said we had to bring the walkie-talkies and wear lifejackets."

"We need a plan once we get to the island," Grace said, settling in between Harvey and Olivia on the backseat of the rowboat, opening her journal. "I'll fill you in on the way over."

"We can't wait to hear. We've been trying to guess all night what this adventure is," Olivia said, her voice flowing like silk, just like her amazing hair. "Your note was so cryptic."

"Yeah, Serpy wants to see us, right?" Harvey asked, looking up at Grace with his glass-green eyes and white-blond hair, a perfect match to his big sister. Harvey was eight and Olivia was nine.

"Yes, and I think it's some other sort of water sprite adventure, but I just couldn't think why you need to go to the island. A new channel maybe?" Olivia asked.

"Here let me show you," Grace responded, opening her journal. She started with the story of

Dougal finding the map and carried on showing them her notes and drawings.

"Dude, you'd better let me do it. You're making us go in circles," Jake demanded from the middle seat, standing up to take over for Cole who had been determined to be in charge of the oars.

Julia, hands gripping the sides of the boat, giggled nervously as the boat rocked and Cole plopped down next to her. Jake got them moving in the right direction.

When they arrived at the island, Julia was the first to climb out. While struggling to lug her overstuffed backpack with her, she began directing the group through grunts, "I think we need to split up," deep breath, pull. "We could use the walkie-talkies to update each other." Grunt, pull. "Pairs of two; Harvey and Cole in the water," rearrange, breath, pull. "Grace and Olivia take the south side of the island and Jake and I will check the..."

Julia gave one last tug with all of her might and her backpack came loose. It flew directly at her knocking her down. Chippy slowly climbed out of the pack onto her face. "North side," she finished.

All of the kids stared at her. She was never the leader at this kind of thing. Playing board games and organizing picnics, yes, but she was never a leader in adventures.

Julia lifted off Chippy, removed her backpack from her chest, sat up, and composed herself. "I think we are looking for another drawing, maybe a carving on a rock, something like that."

The rest of the kids continued to stare at her, trying desperately not to laugh. The contents of her pack were spilling out. The edge of a cookbook, her alligator spray, a pink polar bear, and what looked like Chippy-sized safari clothes. There was even a tiny pair of binoculars.

Jake was the first to move. He didn't care who was in charge, he didn't need an invitation to find the treasure. He took Julia's hand and pulled her up. He took her backpack, shoved the contents back in, and tossed it into the boat. Julia opened her mouth to protest, but thought better of it and followed Jake, leaving a pile of packaging peanuts on the ground where she fell.

Cole and Harvey looked at each other, laughing.

Cole picked up a peanut. "Hey, Julia, what's with these?"

Julia looked back, saw the Styrofoam peanut, and stopped. "Oh, um that. Well that is just a new thing I'm trying. Protection you know." She took the peanut from Cole and tucked it into the back of her jeans. She took a long deep breath and kept walking.

"Right, I see," Cole giggled, shaking his head.

Harvey, still laughing, swept up the pile of foam peanuts still left on the ground, and put them in Julia's backpack.

Cole called back to Grace and Olivia, "We'll check in here in ten minutes underwater time, wait for us and then we can check out the island together." Cole didn't wait for an answer. He jumped into the water and swam off with Loony, Harvey, and Harvey's turtle, Tink.

*****

"So, is your dog your guide or just your pet?" Olivia asked as she and Grace consulted the compass. Olivia looked up at Grace and knew that she had said something wrong.

66

"He's just a dog," Grace sighed. Her eyes immediately began to pool with tears. Obviously everyone knew she didn't have an animal guide, but no one actually came out and talked about it before. "Don't get me wrong, I love Dougal, but everyone else has had an animal guide since the first day and I still

don't. Why don't I have one?" Grace sniffled and the tears that were welling in her eyes began rolling down her cheeks.

"Oh, don't worry Grace. I'm sure your animal guide will be amazing," Olivia said. "You're so organized you haven't even needed a guide. Maybe you won't have one until you really need one."

Olivia's voice was so calm and soothing that Grace was beginning to feel better just listening to her. Maybe Olivia was right. Maybe she just didn't need a guide yet. She wiped her eyes. "Do you really think that's it?"

Olivia smiled, "I know it!"

Grace took a deep breath and smiled too. "Thanks, Olivia. Cole's right, it does seem like we've known you forever." She looked into the water. "Hey, there are the boys. Come on. Let's go find the clue!"

CHAPTER 6
CLUE NUMBER TWO

All of the kids searched their parts of the small island and checked in after ten minutes, but no one had found any sign of the number 2.

Julia was ready with another idea. "Let's go up to the top of that big rock. I think we should be able to see around the whole island from there. We can have a snack and make a new plan." She turned and headed up the hill.

The kids followed. Again, no one made a comment about Julia's newfound assertiveness. When they got to the top, they spread the blanket on the rock and looked around. Julia was right. They could see the whole island from here. They could practically see the whole lake.

"Hey, what's that road?" Jake asked. "It's running off the island right into the lake."

"Wow, that's so cool. It looks like it comes back out again over there," Grace said, opening her journal and making a note.

"I can't see it," Harvey complained, standing on his tip toes. "Boost me up, Cole. I bet I can see if I climb that tree."

"Good idea, Harv," Olivia said, taking Cole's hands to help make a step for Harvey. "See if you can see our camp."

They lifted Harvey into the tree.

"Hey, I can see everything from up here," Harvey shouted, climbing to the highest limb of the sparse, knotty pine tree. "Look there's our camp." He grabbed a new branch and tried to lean out farther.

"Hey, there's a carving up here. It looks like a golf green."

"That's it, it's the clue. I just know it!" Julia cheered, looking up into the tree. "Tell us everything!"

"Wait, I'll give you some paper," Grace said, tearing a piece from her journal. "You can make a rubbing."

"Oh you are so low tech," Jake sneered. "Here just take a picture of it." He pulled a phone from his waterproof pouch and tossed it up to Harvey.

"Brilliant, a phone. Why didn't I think of that with all this sand and water?" Grace fumed through gritted teeth. She handed the paper and pencil up to Harvey and added casually, "Still make a rubbing. It might give us more detail."

Harvey snapped some photos and tossed the phone back to Jake. He leaned farther out to make the rubbing, climbed down, and handed the rubbing to Grace.

"Well, it looks like Cole and I will be finding the next clue," Jake announced with a self-satisfied smile. "Here take a look; it's the golf course all right. And we have our lessons starting tomorrow."

Cole looked over Jake's shoulder. "But which hole is it? I don't see a number on the flag. That golf course is huge."

Olivia nudged Grace. The girls had been studying the rubbing and Grace had begun to outline the darker shaded areas. A very clear 19 showed up on the flag.

"Well, it doesn't make sense," Grace started, "but there actually is a number on the flag. See? A nineteen, right here." She turned the rubbing for the boys to see. With a hand on her hip and eyebrows raised, she added just for Jake, "I guess the old-school way still works."

Jake studied the drawing, looking back to his phone and looking at the drawing again. "Nope, you must have shaded wrong. There's nothing on the flag here on the photo and there are only eighteen holes on the golf course anyway."

"I know that, but this is right," Grace said. "It's perfectly clear. I learned how to make rubbings on the gravestones at my grandma's church."

"Well I don't want to argue with your grandma's crazy church," Jake sniggered. "But even if you know what you're doing, which is *not* what I said, there's no such thing as the nineteenth hole." Jake crossed his arms and stared at Grace.

"Okay, so what do *you* propose?" Grace challenged, crossing her arms and sending her hip out again.

"Well, there is water drawn here, next to the hole. So, I say it's the fourth hole, the one by the pond." Jake smiled.

"Yeah, between the fourth and fifth holes where the trail goes around the pond, that would be a great place for a clue," Cole said, looking at Grace. "Sorry, but it makes more sense than your idea, even if the rubbing is right, it just doesn't make sense." He smiled and added, "Remember the time we saw that painted turtle there when grandpa took us golfing?"

Grace took a deep breath and looked at her brother. "Yeah, I remember and I guess you're right, it would be a good place for a clue. And since you guys start golf lessons tomorrow, you'll be able to check it out."

Jake stepped out of the circle and began to do what looked like a touchdown dance. "Did everyone hear that? Grace just said that I was right! Oh yeah! I never thought that I would see the day when the Great Grace admitted defeat."

Olivia and Harvey, who had been watching the exchange like a beach volleyball match, turned back to Grace.

She began to defend herself. "I didn't say y…" But she stopped herself. It just wasn't worth it.

Olivia rested her arm on Grace's shoulder. She saw the same look on Grace's face that had been there right before she started to cry earlier.

Julia decided it was time to take charge again. "It's picnic time and I made my famous peppermint brownies. I can't wait to find out what the treasure is. Let's make a plan about where to search on the golf course." She had a huge smile on her face as she began walking back toward the blanket, Chippy proudly strutting behind. "And I don't know if you noticed, but I wasn't even scared at all today, not even on the bike."

As Julia walked away, a trail of packaging peanuts fell one by one out of the back of her jeans. All the kids laughed, even Grace.

CHAPTER 7
THE GOLF LESSON

"Check that out. Rock solid par! Take that!" Cole cheered.

They had played the first hole three times already. The instructor didn't seem to notice the group of angry golfers who were lining up behind them. But, he didn't seem to notice that his pink and green plaid shorts didn't exactly match his blue and brown argyle socks and yellow and orange striped shirt either.

"All right golfers, gather in," the instructor called. "I've seen your strokes and I've decided that we're ready to play the whole front nine."

"Yess!" Both boys called out at the same time pumping their fists in the air and giving each other a high five.

"Glad to see the enthusiasm boys," the instructor said, giving them a funny look. He talked out of the side of his mouth, like Popeye without his pipe. He continued on with his speech, "Now remember to lock your pinky and thumb together, keep your eye on the ball and just meet it, don't hit it like a sledge hammer. We don't need any John Bunyans, or is it Henry Paul or no it's Henry Bunyan." He grunted and shook his head. "Either way, no sledge hammers. Got it?"

Jake whispered in Cole's ear, "I bet I beat you every hole."

Cole rubbed his hands together, a smile creeping onto his face. "Let's make this interesting, one ball per hole. You win, I get your ball; I win, you get mine."

"Dude, that's not fair. I only have four balls. My grandpa forgot to get me new ones," Jake complained, trying to think of a better wager.

"Oh well, I guess you'd better win then," Cole said, taking off after the instructor, who had just called his name to join the first foursome teeing off. He turned around to Jake. "Good luck! I'll take it easy on you this hole."

Cole set his ball on the tee. It was the water hole, over the pond. The golfers who had been impatiently waiting at the first hole were now practically breathing down his back. This was his time to shine. If he wacked the ball as hard as he could, he would totally show Jake how much better he had gotten, and those golfers would be so impressed they might ask him to join the league or something. He lined up his feet, linked his pinky with his thumb, pulled back the club as far as he could, and swung it down as fast and hard as possible. The ball went flying! It just missed the instructor's head and continued on across the bog and into the pond, at a complete right angle from the hole. He sliced it.

"Now that's why I always remind you to just meet the ball, not hit it like a sledge hammer," the instructor scolded and turned to call the next kid, "Caleb, up to the tee."

The men behind him were humphing, tisking, and snickering and Jake was full out laughing, but Cole saw this as the perfect opportunity. Caleb was a terrible golfer, or at least he was pretending to be. He was Danish, so Cole didn't know what he and his brother were actually saying to each other, but it sure seemed like they were just making fun of the instructor. Caleb always knocked the ball off the tee at least five times before hitting it.

Cole cleared his throat, "Excuse me, sir, sorry about that *John Henry*, but that was my last ball so could I just look for some in the woods and meet up with you at the end of the hole?"

The instructor mumbled, "Yes, yes, John Henry that's it." Then he added, "What? Sir? I am not a sir. Call me Mr. Bob. And yeah, sure, go find your ball." Mr. Bob grunted, standing up from putting the ball back on the tee, after Caleb once again *accidentally* knocked it off. His brother, Lukas, was laughing and saying something in Danish that sounded a lot like "do it again."

Cole grabbed Jake's arm and quietly added, "I don't want to get lost. I'd better bring someone with me."

The boys took off through the boggy area toward the woods. They ran, dodging trees, trying to make it to the trail as quickly as possible to start the search.

"One of us better check the water before the group catches up," Cole panted. "And the other one can check the trail."

"I call the water and I'm getting some golf balls while I'm down there," Jake said, wading farther into the bog, holding his glowing fairy stone pouch in his hand.

"Good idea, there must be thousands in there. My uncle used to find them and sell them. Maybe we could try that," Cole said, doing the math in his head. If they charged twenty-five cents a ball, and found one hundred balls, that would be like twenty-five dollars. He could buy loads of stuff at the sprite stores or maybe they could even save up and go to Sprite Slide World.

"Right, I'll meet you back on the trail by the fourth hole. I'll check the whole pond," Jake said, treading farther into the murky water. "I sure hope the light works in there, it's so goopy on the bottom."

Cole headed back into the woods thinking that it would be handy if time could stay still for him too, but luckily Chippy showed up to help him. He weaved back and forth searching the woods for the clue. All that he found were golf balls. He had to make a pouch out of the front of his shirt to hold all of them.

When he made it back to the end of the path, Jake was standing by the water pump, hardly recognizable through the mud and slime that was covering him. He had a ladle in his hand.

"Dude, that was disgusting. Look at me," Jake groaned, mud hanging from every inch of him. Every hair on his arms and legs was covered with a black slime. It looked like he had fur. "How am I going to explain this?"

"Nasty, you smell disgusting too. Could you see anything down there?" Cole asked, holding his nose.

"It's only a few feet deep and the water was clear, but there must be ten feet of slime and gunk on the bottom. I tried to sift through it, but all I found were these golf balls and a few turtles." Jake looked down at the ground where there was a pile of slime covered balls and two turtles struggling to climb over the miniature muddy mountains.

Cole laughed. "Come on, give me the ladle." He pumped the handle up and down until the water started to flow. He caught the water in a ladle and began dumping it over Jake's head.

"Hurry up, that water is freezing," Jake complained, his knees knocking together as he covered the front of his body with his arms to protect it from the cold.

"Stop being such a baby," Cole laughed. Watching Jake squirm was even better than beating him with a great drive. "Here comes the group." Cole was truly enjoying himself now.

The group and the instructor approached the boys walking slower and slower trying to figure out what was going on.

"Just fell in the pond trying to reach a ball that's all. Nothing to see here, move along." Jake smiled

trying to make it look like it was no big deal, him standing there soaking wet, bits of slime and pond scum still hanging from his ears and hair.

"My, my, boys, you have been busy. Hurry up and wash up, Jake. Cole, I see you found some balls." Mr. Bob looked at the collection of balls that Cole had dumped near his feet. "You've got some nice ones there. And wow, that's an oldie, I don't think you'll want to be playing with that one." Mr. Bob bent down to pick up the ball, light blue boxer shorts with monkeys all over them were sticking out of the top of his pink and green shorts, perfectly completing his crazy outfit. He examined the ball. "Don't hit very far, those. The Nineteenth Hole, I wonder who the jokester was who came up with that name. If you're using *this* ball, you'll definitely need a drink at the end of the game."

Cole and Jake looked at each other. The nineteenth hole?

"Jake are these yours?" Mr. Bob continued, pointing to a pile of slimy black balls. "They won't be any good; waterlogged." He tossed Cole the Nineteenth Hole ball and began walking down the path, adding, "Put a move on boys."

Cole stared at the ball. The Nineteenth Hole, that was it, Grace was right. There was a Nineteenth Hole. "Excuse me, sir, I mean, Mr. Bob!" Cole called. "What's the Nineteenth Hole?"

"Well it's the clubhouse, young man. But I suppose you wouldn't know that would you? Yep, when you get old like me, you really look forward to the Nineteenth Hole." Mr. Bob smiled to himself and turned to walk away, mumbling, "Especially after trying to teach a bunch of coconuts like the lot of you."

Cole was too excited to be offended. "Hey Jake, this is it. Look, it says the Nineteenth Hole, Dakotis Club. There was a sign for that club in Lake Champlain."

Jake didn't get a chance to respond because Caleb and Lukas, who had been given the job of carrying Cole's and Jake's bags, dropped them on the wet path in front of the pump, right in the slimiest part.

"Hey, thanks a lot," Jake griped. "Ya didn't have to drop it right in the mud, ya know."

Cole picked up the ladle of cold water and poured it over Jake's head again.

Caleb and Lukas looked at Jake and then back at Cole. They looked at each other and began backing away, heading toward the first hole, whispering in a flurry of mixed Danish and English. Cole was sure that he heard the words *water sprite* and *monster* and *Dakotis Club*. Then they turned and ran.

"Dudes, what's your problem? Are you afraid of a little slime?" Jake hollered, wiping his eyes clean. The skin underneath wasn't just clean, it was glowing.

"No, I think they might be scared of us. Look, we're glowing," Cole said, holding up his arm. It was sparkling in the water, like it was made of thousands of little diamonds, reflecting light in every direction. He added, "And I think they might know that we're sprites. Come on, you're never going to be clean. Let's just say we have to go home. Maybe we can follow them." Cole picked up their bags and started jogging to catch up to Mr. Bob.

CHAPTER 8
THE NINETEENTH HOLE

"I still can't believe that we'd never heard of the Nineteenth Hole," Grace said to Cole as the group swam together through Lake George.

"I know. You'd think Grandpa would be all over that one. He's always taking us in for a drink after we golf," Cole agreed, then looked over at Jake. "Do you see it yet?"

"Yeah, right up there," Jake said, pointing up ahead to an old stone tunnel tucked into an underwater hillside. "I love this channel. We've got to find a way to get that undersurf board."

"I hate this channel," Julia whined. She closed her eyes and began her new underwater calming technique, blowing streams of tiny bubbles.

"Oh, you've been fine the last five times we've gone to Lake Champlain," Grace said, laughing. "It was only that first time that you nearly lost your bathing suit top."

Julia finished blowing out a line of bubbles and smiled. "And I will never wear a bikini in a river channel again!"

"Well, thank you," Jake sniggered, "Cause, that wasn't fun for any of us!" He turned his attention back to the channel. "I'm gonna try to catch an aerial off this mama and I'll meet you at the Dakotis Club."

"Just remember, Julia, feet first and you can just sit and ride the wave," Cole advised. "Come on, I really want to see this golf course. And who knows, maybe we'll even figure out how to make it into the Atlantic Channel."

The boys had discovered signs leading to the Atlantic Ocean when they brought a lost sea serpent back to Lake Champlain in the beginning of the summer. But every time the kids made it to the channel, one of them wimped out.

First it was Grace who worried that she didn't study the maps enough and they wouldn't be able to get home. Then Cole thought he saw a black jelly fish watching them near the entrance. Harvey and Olivia didn't think they should risk going without the animal guides, and even though they had seen some salt water animals in fresh water, that didn't mean the fresh water animals could be in salt water.

Julia never even wanted to go in the first place, so she was always ready to turn around and head home. And Jake who had always been gung ho, ready to explore the bigger waves and meet more mermaids, had even shied away from the channel after his dad had called him last week.

His dad was a marine wildlife specialist who was a treasure hunter in his spare time. He had told Jake that there had been a particularly dubious group of treasure hunters who had been disturbing some fragile coral and other endangered species. He had said that they were dangerous; that they were being called deep sea pirates because they were not just protecting their own finds, but they were stealing other people's treasure as well. And they had even disconnected the air supply of these two scuba divers who had gotten too close. The divers had only just made it back to the surface alive.

Jake's dad gave him a book every summer when he said good-bye at the airport. The books were about sunken ships, missing cities, the history of treasure hunting, and books about pirates. Jake had always tucked the book in his backpack in California

93

and as soon as he arrived in the Adirondacks he added it to the ever-growing stack next to his camp bed. And there they sat, nine unopened books, one for each summer his dad had shipped him off to his grandparents.

Every year, he thought maybe his grandma would clear them out, but every year they greeted him like a reminder that his mom was gone. Jake's dad insisted that he come to camp every year because that's what his mom would have wanted. If his dad cared so much about what she wanted, why did he let her leave?

But after the phone conversation about the pirates, Jake had actually decided maybe it was time to read the books. And they were a little thrilling, but a little scary too. Some of these treasure hunters would do anything to protect their find, and there were a lot of missing treasures still to be found. Including sunken ships off the east coast, and who knew where the channel would come out.

So, without any more discussion, the kids had just been avoiding the Atlantic Channel altogether.

When they arrived at the Dakotis Club, they were greeted with lots of people staring, pointing, and smiling at them.

A little girl about four years old came tearing across the first green, wearing a giant smile, yelling "It's them, it's them. I want to see."

An older girl and two boys watched from the green. The girls had matching yellow sundress bathing suits and matching long brown hair with perfectly straight bangs. The older one called out, "Mali, you mustn't. It might not be safe." But the little girl kept running all the way up to Cole and Jake. She stood at their feet looking up at them with an expectant smile.

The older girl, who must have been about the same age as Jake and Cole, caught up with Mali and began to pull at her arm trying to get her away. "Mali, you must stop it now. Mummy and Daddy will be very cross." The older sister gave Mali a look that clearly meant, "Don't say another word and come with me or I'll never bring you with me again."

Mali seemed to understand the look because she let her sister take her hand. She continued to look at the boys as she was dragged backward, saying, "But

Leywa, they don't look strong enough to kill a monster."

Leywa staggered, trying to cover her sister's mouth with her free hand. She gave the boys a slight giggle and nod in apology. Jake and Cole watched the exchange like it was a TV show. They just stood like statues as amazed by the little girl as she seemed to be by them.

"What was that all about?" Harvey asked when the girls made it back to the green, Mali still being dragged backward so she could watch them. "Do you know them?"

"No, but who does she think she is, saying we don't look strong enough to kill a monster?" Jake asked, looking at Mali, flexing his muscles, and loudly growling, "I am plenty strong enough to kill a monster."

Mali shrieked from out on the golf course.

"I know, right, I mean seriously," Cole agreed, flexing his biceps and grunting. "We're fierce!" This time a few of the small kids nearby shrieked and looked for places to hide.

"Oh, stop it. You're scaring them," Grace said, pulling out her journal and starting to sketch. "Did those boys look familiar?" she asked.

"Actually yeah, I was thinking that they looked like those Danish kids from the golf lesson," Cole said, waving to a little boy in apology. The boy saw that Cole was looking at him and his eyes opened so wide so fast that they looked like they were ready to pop right out of his head.

Grace turned the journal toward the kids. She showed them the sketch she had just drawn and then turned back a few pages and showed them a nearly matching sketch. "This is what I drew when I asked you to describe them yesterday. Look, they're identical."

"It kind of seems like everyone knows you around here," Olivia said, looking around at all of the sprites and merpeople still watching them.

"Oh no," Julia worried, beginning to blow little streams of bubbles again. "This isn't good. Why do they know you and why are those boys following you?"

CHAPTER 9
THE TREASURE BOX

"You don't think they mean Serpy when they keep saying monster, do you?" Julia asked, adjusting her goggles.

Jake laughed. "How would *they* know about Serpy?"

Grace looked at Cole. "Did anyone see you when you guys were rescuing him?"

Cole bit his lip, thinking. "Um, no, I don't think so." A huge smiled crossed his face and he added, "except for those reporters." He laughed and high-fived Jake.

"Yeah, the scaredy-cats. But there's no way they knew who we were," Jake added.

"What about the merpeople in Lake Champlain?" Julia asked. "Or maybe someone saw you in the other lakes?"

"I really don't think so," Cole said, "but I guess they could have. I mean there were a lot of sprites at that carnival, one of them might have seen us."

"Well by the looks you're getting, and the attention from those boys at the golf course and now these girls, someone knows something," Grace said.

"Cole, do you realize what this means? We're heroes!" Jake smiled and waved to the golfers. Some people smiled back, others gave him strange looks, and a little boy actually hid behind an older boy.

"I don't know about that. They aren't exactly cheering for us, are they?" Cole asked.

Grace pulled at Jake's waving arm. "No, they aren't. Check out that guy." She looked toward the clubhouse where there was a man with long, dark hair watching them.

All of the kids turned to see and the man didn't even look away. He just continued to stare at them with his dark eyes. His jaw was square and set with the tension visible in his cheeks. He had thick black eyebrows and some sort of claw was hanging from his neck.

Julia started her little bubbles again. "Let's just focus," bubbles, "on the clue," bubbles, "not that guy," bubbles, and then pointing to the left and more bubbles, "or that guy."

The kids followed her finger, looking to the left and saw another man ducking into the clubhouse.

Grace took Julia's hand. "Yeah, let's focus on the Nineteenth Hole and finding the treasure."

"Okay, but this club shop isn't called the Nineteenth Hole," Olivia said. "Look, it's called the

Treasure Box."

Grace's eyes lit up. "The Treasure Box, that's it! We found it!"

Jake snorted and looked at Grace. "Don't you get it? It's just a cruel joke. *This* is the treasure," he sighed, pointing at the golf club's store, "a crumbly old shop."

Everyone's smiles slowly fell, along with their shoulders, realizing what Jake was saying. This was it? This was the treasure? They had been so excited and this was the treasure? A golf club shop?

Everyone that is, except for Grace. Grace's smile grew even bigger. "Don't listen to him, this is it, you guys. Uncle Kevin must have hidden the treasure in the club shop. I mean come on, what better place to hide a treasure than in the *Treasure Box*?" Grace challenged, raising her eyebrows and looking at her friends. "Come on, it's got to be in there somewhere."

Grace pulled out her journal and swam off toward the shop.

"Wait, what about the guy I saw?" Julia asked.

"Come on, you were right. Let's just focus on the treasure. That guy was probably just watching us because Jake was acting weird," Grace offered.

Cole clapped Grace on the back, relieved. "Good thinking, the treasure *inside* the treasure box." They swam together into the Treasure Box. "Now the question is: Where is the treasure?"

Jake glared at Grace as he followed up the end of the line.

Cole swam up to the desk where an elderly merman was helping measure out clubs for a young sprite girl. "Excuse me sir, but have you ever heard of Motion Fresh?"

The merman dropped the club he was holding and looked at Cole, a wide smile spread across his face. He scanned the other kids' faces, nodding his head as he looked at each one. He returned his gaze to Cole. "I was wondering when you'd be back. It just hasn't been the same around here without you." He continued to nod his head and smile. "Your locker is full, just like you left it. It was a good idea making that moose lock."

Cole was about to speak up to explain that the merman must be mistaking him with someone else, but Grace nudged him.

The merman continued, "No one has been able to get into it. Not even your buddy when he came last week." He smiled again and opened the half wall that led behind the desk. "I'd hurry now, he was pretty mad and he's been lurking around ever since we saw you on Sees All Updates."

CHAPTER 10
LOCKER NUMBER 34

The kids scrambled through the wall. They entered a maze of hallways with doors leading off each side. Most of them were labeled: men's room, ladies' room, sprite supply cupboard, locker room, grounds supplies.

Cole was first. He could hear Jake behind him complaining.

"What was he talking about? I've never been here before. And what the heck is a Sees All Update?" Cole panicked knowing all the kids thought he came without them. "And what locker is he talking about?"

"Nice try, Cole," Jake grunted. "You've obviously already been here before looking for the treasure."

"And when do you think I would've done that? I've been with you guys all summer long!" Cole shouted at Jake.

"Wait," Grace whispered, looking at a poster hanging on the wall. "It wasn't you. Look, you guys. It was Uncle Kevin."

On the poster stood Cole or at least the boy looked just like Cole. He was doing a headstand and there was trophy on his feet. There was another boy next to him helping to hold the trophy.

Grace took the picture off the wall. There was a golden tag tacked to the frame. She read it out. "Winners of the Freedom Day Dolphin Tournament and Dance Competition three years running: Motion Fresh."

Jake grabbed the photograph. "This is it, I knew it. The treasure is here somewhere. Thank you Motion Fresh. Oh yeah, and sorry dude, I guess you do look a lot like your uncle. But I didn't know that, did I?"

"Um, and that man I saw outside earlier, he looks a lot like that other Motion Fresh guy," Julia stuttered. "Come on we've got to hurry up." She opened the door marked locker room.

The kids quickly followed her, entering a room full of wall-length lockers made out of the insides of giant oyster shells. They were smooth and shiny and iridescent, constantly changing colors. The room was beautiful. It had a high glass ceiling that let the sunlight come in stripes into the room. The lockers were an ever-changing rainbow of color; the rainbow leading them right to the treasure.

"Look they all end there," Harvey sang, pointing to a locker in the middle of the back row.

"No, dude, they end over there," Jake challenged, pointing at the actual end of the lockers.

"No, he means the rainbows all end there," Olivia clarified, swimming toward the locker.

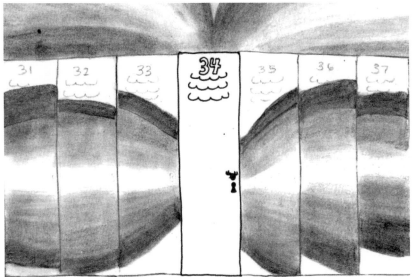

"Oh, it's beautiful," Julia whispered, pulling on Grace, who was drawing and writing in the notebook, trying to copy the photograph, and draw the whole room and remember the exact words the merman said, and describe the men who were looking at them.

Cole was already at the locker. "It's number 34, this is definitely it. The 3 and the 4 on the map were supposed to be together. I just knew if Kevin spent this much time on the map he wouldn't forget the comma."

"Well open it already!" Jake demanded.

Grace had been keeping the clubhouse Moose Key in her fairy stone pouch. She opened the pouch, fit the moose and the key into the lock, and turned.

The door opened into a shell-lined room that must have filled the space behind most of the lockers. There was a stone table and two chairs in the middle. Grace swam over to the table and picked up a pile of papers.

Cole headed straight for a pile of sea-leather bags that were stacked up in the corner. He reached into one and pulled out a handful of colorful shiny coins of all different sizes, the largest was as big as the bottom of a sand bucket and the smallest was the size of a mini marshmallow.

The rest of the kids followed him, each taking a bag full of coins. Jake sank to the ground, picked the bag up over his head and let the coins float down over his face.

"Oh my gosh, you guys," Grace said, looking up from the papers. "Look at this." Grace held up another map. It showed the Dakotis Club and a river channel leading straight from the fairy circle at camp. Attached to it was a note. Grace read out loud:

Congratulations! You found my treasure! I am sorry to inform you that this treasure comes with a price. I made the money finding and selling golf balls. My friend Pierre and I had a plan to make it to the National Break Dancing Competition— Michael Jackson was going to be there. But then we found our stones and we found this club. We started our own competition and we always won. Everyone knew us and everyone loved us. We had fans all over the underwater world. Then our money started disappearing. Pierre had been acting weird for a while and I'm sure it was him. So, I thought of the map. I paid for a Route Chute from the locker to camp and I changed all of the locks so Pierre couldn't get to the money anymore. I am heading home tomorrow and I doubt I'll be back. This is my third summer and all the sprites I know lost the magic after their third summer. Now, you have the treasure, but you also have the responsibility to find out what Pierre was planning with this money.

Jake pulled the map away from Grace. "No way! You mean we could have found this on the first day of summer?" Jake used his free hand to pick up the coins and let them fall through his hands into a pile on the stone table. "I can finally go to the Surf's Down shop."

"Except we don't know if they're worth anything anywhere," Grace said, waking Jake from his dreams of luxurious purchases.

"What do you mean? Dakotis coins? They're what sprites use to pay for all that awesome stuff in the shops." Jake stared at Grace as though she were a complete idiot. "You can't tell me, Miss Notebook, Miss I-know-everything, that you didn't notice all the signs in the stores saying Dakotis coins only," Jake laughed, looking at Grace with a smug smile.

Grace deflated, like she had been punched in the stomach. She didn't mean to be a know it all, but if she knew something why not speak up? And if she left the planning to Jake he would still be in the clubhouse oogling pictures of sea monsters and mermaids. But he was right, she didn't notice the signs. How could she not notice the signs?

She even knows who Dakota and Otis were. She read all about them in the *Sprites in History* book she found in the clubhouse. How when their parents died, and they had no other family, they decided to stay in the underwater world to work as diplomats with the above-water authorities. She had even read how they had set up the Dakotis aquatic monetary system for the underwater world. How could she have missed it?

Jake looked smug. "What, I finally made you speechless?" He sniggered, "Well, I never thought I'd see the day when the great Grace was speechless."

Grace felt a lump growing in her throat. No, she wasn't going to cry. He could be mean, but she wasn't going to let him see her cry. Maybe he was right, maybe if she didn't stick her nose in so much he would have his stupid surf board, then he could just, he could just, surf all the time. She turned her back and took a deep breath, pushing the lump out of her throat. "Well you heard him, what're we waiting for, let's go buy some stuff!"

"Wait, shouldn't we count the money first and make a plan how we spend it or something?" Julia prompted, staring at Grace like she had three heads.

Cole, Olivia, and Harvey all moved forward at the same time reaching for the notebook.

Cole spoke first, "Yeah, slow down, Sis. If there's someone out there looking for me, I'm not just gonna be out there willy-nilly spending the guy's money."

Olivia spread the notebook on the table rereading the note. "I agree. We need to make a plan."

"Well apparently I plan too much, so I say let's just have a free-for-all and see how far that gets us. Jake, did you fill your pockets yet?" Grace snapped, giving him a horrible look.

"Jeez, Grace, I'm sorry, but you are bossy sometimes," Jake responded, returning the nasty look.

Julia stood up, placing her hands on her hips. "Jake, just because she's smart and makes sure there's a plan it doesn't mean she's bossy. You would still be lost in the Chain Lakes, without Mikey I might add, if it weren't for Grace." She dropped her arms and swam right up to Jake, poked him in the chest, and added, "So don't be such a meany!"

Cole and Harvey looked from the girls to Jake.

"It's probably best if we count the money and record it before we go spending it," Harvey suggested. "Grace, maybe you could write it down," he hinted, tapping on the notebook.

"Well, actually," Olivia said, looking up from the notebook. "It looks like your uncle Kevin kept pretty good track of the money. That is as long as it's all still here." Olivia flipped the page and the kids saw the accounting tallies of all the different coins and as their eyes traveled down the page to the total amount, they couldn't believe it. Right at the bottom of the page it said "9/7/1981-grand total-$2,450.63."

"We're rich. I want to buy one of those cool swim headbands," Julia declared, pushing her hair back, her bangs floating softly off her forehead and the rest of her hair still floating in front of her eyes. "I got the goggles so I could see, but now I can't see through my hair and I just don't look good in ponytails."

"I'm gonna check out those foot surf boards."
Jake looked at Cole and Harvey. "Right, dudes?"

"Yeah and I want to get some of those underwater golf clubs too," Cole added.

"What about that candy store?" Harvey asked, smiling just thinking of all the new types of candies that he had seen.

Grace hesitantly joined the conversation, "I wonder if we should start with buying the things that we need. Like the underwater GPS and Light in All Darkness flashlight and things like that." She looked around the group, watching for signs that she was sounding too bossy. But all of the kids including Jake agreed and actually began adding to the list of essentials.

"And a Bounteous Bag. We can bring everything in it," Julia said

"Don't forget those Takes the Time energy drinks," Cole suggested.

"And we should get more map books," Grace added.

"Yeah, I can check out the Pacific this winter, I go to the beach all the time," Jake said, rubbing his hand through his hair.

"I might go to Jamaica this year," Julia mumbled. "But there is no way I'm exploring underwater without you guys."

Grace turned to Harvey and Olivia. "What about you guys? Any vacation plans this winter?"

Olivia looked at Harvey, not sure what to say. "Well, we never really know where we're going to be. Our mom and dad just told us last night that we might be moving again. Our dad's just been offered a new assignment in Africa somewhere. They said we might not even be able to come back here next year." Olivia looked at all of her camp friends. "Sorry, we should've told you before, but we're just really hoping that it's not true."

Julia ran up to Olivia and then Harvey and hugged them both. "Oh you have to come back. You just have to."

"What? You can't not be here!" Cole shouted and stopped himself. "I mean wow, it would really stink if you're not here next summer," he sighed, looking at Harvey and then stared at Olivia, trying to stop the panic that was beginning to creep into his stomach.

"Well, we know we have one more week before school starts, so let's stop worrying about the future and enjoy shopping," Grace said, not sure how to handle this. "You'll be back even if it's not next summer."

"Yeah, you're right. There's no point thinking too much about it since there's nothing we can do about it." Harvey shrugged his shoulders. "Let's go. Maybe we could even check out those foot boards before we leave."

"I can't believe that I have to go back to school in a few days. I don't want to leave. This summer has been so great," Julia sniffed, her eyes puddling with tears.

"Well I hate to tell you this, but I leave tomorrow," Jake announced. He carried on, playing with the money, acting like it was no big deal. All of the kids dropped what they were doing and stared at him.

"What? But school doesn't start until next week," Cole complained. "Why didn't you tell us this before?"

"Hate to break it to you, but school started *last* week in California. The only reason I'm still here is because my uncle is getting married this weekend. We leave tomorrow morning for Syracuse and then I head home."

Jake swam away, leaving the rest of the kids staring after him speechless.

CHAPTER 11
MR. SNYDER

Grace counted the money and they headed out through the Treasure Box shop.

"Thanks, sir, you were right, it was all there," Cole said to the merman at the desk. "What was your name again?"

"Mr. Snyder. Originally from the North Sea, but just too cold there now, so I travel with the summer fairs here in the Northern American waters and then I head to the Mediterranean for the winter. Not a bad life really."

"Wow, I would love to go to the Medi-terranean," Julia interrupted, thinking of the great food and clothes in Europe. Then she shivered and asked, "Is it hard to get across the Atlantic?"

"Just takes some getting used to that's all. When you try it, stick to the currents. You don't want to lose the currents. That's a big ocean. One time when my family was going to visit the Caribbean Gulf for a vacation, my brother accidentally pushed me out of the current and I was lost for days. My family was gone just like that.

"Don't get me wrong, it was amazing. No one ever believed me, but I found Atlantis. A golden city, right on a southern ridge of the Mid-Atlantic Mountains. Yep, tucked right into the side of the mountain, like what you guys have above water, Machu Picchu. There were all sorts of amazing sea animals there." Mr. Snyder smiled. "It was beautiful, but thankfully I finally found the Canary Current which led me to the North Equatorial Current and I made it back to the Gulf and to my family."

"Wow, did you ever try to find it again?" Grace asked.

"Well now, believe me, I tried. I nearly had it narrowed down too. I was keeping a map, crossing off all the places that I looked. I even showed it to your buddy Pierre. He was very interested too." Mr. Snyder said, looking at Cole. "Actually, he became obsessed with it. Then my map disappeared and I never had another question from him." Mr. Snyder laughed. "But then we never saw him again did we? Until last week that is."

"Did he say he was looking for Cole, I mean Kevin?" Grace asked.

"No, just straight to the locker," Mr. Snyder said. "He pushed right past me, no hello or anything. It took me a minute to figure out who he was; I'm not used to seeing sprites when they're old. Boy was he mad when he left."

"Wait, he was old? But how can he come here if he is old?" Julia asked.

"Oh I see an old sprite every once in a while. I just figured they never lost the magic for some reason. Either way, Kevin, you'd better watch your back," Mr. Snyder warned, "Like I said, he was mad."

"Yeah, um, thanks for the warning," Cole sighed, turning away from Mr. Snyder and mumbling to his friends. "I think we should go shopping." He swam out of the shop.

"Maybe we should get you a disguise," Harvey suggested, swimming after Cole. "I mean if Pierre is old like your uncle he's probably not really looking for a young Kevin unless he sees one."

"Dudes, enough of this nonsense. No one is looking for you, Cole. That guy Mr. Snyder is like a hundred years old. He doesn't know what he's talking about. I mean have you ever seen adult sprites?" Jake waited, glaring at all of his friends. No one responded.

"That's what I thought. I'm heading straight to the surf shop. Join me if you want," he declared, turning and swimming toward the Surf's Down shop.

"Hey wait up, I want to come too," Cole called, shaking his head, his shaggy hair moving in waves carrying away his doubts. He swam to catch Jake. "I mean, you're right, why would anyone want anything from me? I don't even know anyone down here."

"Remember, we're trying to get all of the things on the list first," Grace moaned, annoyed that she had to be the boring annoying one again. "And Harvey's right. We should get a hat or something for Cole."

Cole slowed down, turned, and swam over to Grace. He called to Jake, "Come on Jake, she's right. We agreed to get the stuff we need first. And those DeAndre's Dry Swim Caps *are* pretty cool."

Jake stopped, clenched his fists, tensed his whole body, let out a low growl, and finally turned around to join the group. He glared at Grace.

Harvey quickly stepped in front of Jake. "It looks like we can get most of the things we need at the Underwater Gadgets store, so why don't we start there?" He suggested extra cheerfully.

"Sounds good, let's go," Julia said, taking Jake's hand, not giving him a chance to head in another direction.

CHAPTER 12
GADGETS

The kids swam through the underwater streets, nodding greetings of hello to the other sprites they passed. They couldn't help but wonder where they all came from. Everyone they passed looked like they could be from a different country. The hairstyles, bathing suits, languages, they were all different. And the merpeople running the stores usually didn't even speak English.

But still, the kids knew they were being watched and talked about. Julia was sure she even saw people pointing at them.

"Hey you guys, I can't ignore everyone staring at us. It's freaking me out," Julia squeaked, holding onto Jake's hand just a little tighter.

"Oh don't worry, they're probably just noticing Grace's hair, people notice her everywhere we go," Cole offered with a shaky, unconvincing voice, as he pushed the door open to the Underwater Gadgets shop.

"Yeah, people always stare at us too. Even stop to touch our hair sometimes," Harvey added, smiling an uncertain smile at Olivia, who had also noticed how many red and white-blond haired mermaids there were.

"I guess, but they're all staring at the boys," Julia muttered quietly enough that no one felt the need to respond.

The kids all piled into the store, quickly diverting their attention to the many cool gadgets for sale. They consulted the list and began wandering through the store collecting things.

Cole, Jake, and Harvey stuck together trying to scope out useful surfing gadgets, like Current Compasses with built-in thermometers and speed indicators, Wavy Wax, and Fabulous Fins. They were just turning the corner into the area where DeAndre's

DEANDRE'S DRY SWIM CAPS

Dry Swim Caps were kept when they saw four sets of eyes looking out from behind a potted coral.

"Dude, don't look now, but I think we're being watched again," Jake breathed without moving his lips. He tried hard to scope the area without moving his head. Cole and Harvey did the same.

Just then one set of eyes moved forward, and Mali, the little girl from the golf course, came swimming out pointing a finger at Jake and Harvey. "But who are they? They're not the other boy on the poster." Leywa reached out and pulled her sister back.

"It's the girls from the golf course and those Danish boys again," Cole whispered back.

"Yeah, what do they want with us? They can't seriously know it was us in that picture in the paper saving Serpy," Jake griped a little too loudly causing Caleb and Lukas to look in their direction. Jake couldn't stand these guys getting in the way of his undersurf board. "What?" he blurted. "What do you want from us?"

Mali shrieked and waved, Leywa stared, Lukas put his hands on his hips, and Caleb, the older boy, stepped in front of the other three like he needed to

protect them. He quickly led the kids toward the door and hurried them out of the shop, continuing to look over his shoulder, like he was expecting to be followed.

Jake shrugged his shoulders. "Well I guess that gets rid of them. Now, on to my surfing gear."

"Um, what did she mean? What poster?" Harvey asked. "This is getting too weird."

"You're not kidding. Let's find the girls and get out of here," Cole agreed, ignoring Jake's immediate complaints, and grabbing a blue spiky swim cap from the rack as he headed toward the girls in the underwater GPS section of the store.

Grace was holding a round, clear ball. It had two needles inside, one pointing straight up and the other pointing to the right. "All right, we've gotten everything on our list. This Which Way Up compass was a great idea and this current detector might really come in helpful when we go in the ocean," Grace said, checking off all of the items that were listed in the notebook.

"Perfect, *now* can I go get my undersurf board?" Jake snarled.

Grace took a deep breath, trying to ignore Jake, and continued. "Anyway, as I was saying, we have eighty-five extra dollars in Dakotis coins, and I was thinking we could split it so we could each choose our own things. What do you think?"

"That would be what, about fourteen dollars each. Or should we do twelve each and put the thirteen extra dollars back into the budget?" Olivia asked, quickly doing the math. Then she reached out and picked up a small oval ball. "Or, maybe we could use the money to buy the Sees All communication system. It might be really useful to always know where we all are."

"Yeah, that would have been handy when we lost Mikey," Cole laughed, thinking of the time that he had lost his cousin in a river channel. "How do they work?"

"Well, it says here," Olivia read from the tag, "Sees All communication systems can link you up with friends and family. Just sync your Sees All hub to any other short wave system and you're connected!" Olivia looked up. "It sounds like we could always know when and where everyone is swimming."

"Yeah, and then we could all kind of keep in touch over the winter," Harvey added. "And if Olivia and I end up staying in Africa next summer, we could still see what you guys are doing."

"That's it. We have to buy them. How much are they?" Julia asked with a look of panic. The idea of all the kids being separated for the winter was hard enough, but to think that they might not be together next summer was just unimaginable.

Olivia smiled, "That's just it, for all of us to align our stones and for each of us to get our own Sees

All hub we would need the rest of the money. So we would all have to agree, and Jake you wouldn't be able to buy your surfing gear."

"Dudes, can't we just e-mail or something? You know I really had my heart set on that board."

"Well, you could e-mail, but if Harvey and I end up in Africa we might not have any access to the Internet." Olivia was trying to sound uplifting, but the look in her green eyes couldn't hide her disappointment. "So, I guess we could just catch up when we get back, whenever that might be." She looked at the kids, lingering on Cole for just a second longer than the others.

"Well, that's just ridiculous, if Jake doesn't want to be a part of it, he doesn't have to. He can ride his surf board while we keep in touch. I say we do it." Grace put her hand in the middle. "Water sprites have to stick together. What do you say?"

Cole put his hand on top of Grace's. "I'm in."

Julia added her hand. "Definitely!" she shouted, giving Jake a pleading look.

"Thanks guys," Harvey said, adding his hand to the pile followed by a smiling Olivia.

"Yeah all right, I get it, the board can wait." Jake reluctantly added his hand to the pile, again giving Grace a horrible look.

Grace turned away from Jake, took another deep breath, and said "One, two, three." Together all of the kids called out "Water Sprites!" some showing more enthusiasm than others.

*****

The camp kids made their purchases and swam back to the Dakotis Club.

Grace was at the back of the line and she was just about to enter the Treasure Box when she felt a tug on the back of her new Bounteous Bag.

Grace turned and Leywa was there holding out a rolled-up piece of paper, her hand shaking.

Grace took the paper. "Um, thanks."

"I thought you should know," she said with a jittery voice. "If he was my friend I would want to know. I mean he's so amazing, right? Why would anyone do this?"

Grace didn't know what to say. Who was so amazing? "Um, yeah, thanks again." She tucked the rolled paper in the Bounteous Bag. "I, um, better go."

"Yes, okay. Say hi to him for me, okay? And tell him we're taking the rest of those down." She pointed at the rolled paper. "Look out for him. I mean, I can't believe I've actually seen him. I've had a poster of him on my wall at home since I first found my stone. He's just so dreamy."

"Uh, okay, yeah. I'll tell him. But, I'd better go," Grace turned to leave. "Thanks again." She waved to Leywa and swam into the Treasure Box.

*****

Grace entered the rainbow room to a flurry of talking and people handing her the notebooks and maps to put into the Bounteous Bag. Cole and Grace's uncle Kevin had not only left them the money, he had also left notes on "How to make the most money selling your golf balls." He even included maps of the best places to find the balls.

Cole and Julia had already made a plan to come back golf ball hunting and the group excitedly told Grace the plans to make more money in the last few days at camp. They figured if Grace, Cole, and Julia worked hard enough, they might make enough money for the group to finally go to Sprite Slide World next summer. And maybe they could find out more about Uncle Kevin and his ex-friend, Pierre.

They all agreed to keep any money they earned in the Treasure Box and to not spend it without consulting one another.

The water sprites entered the Route Chute that led back to camp according to Kevin's map. It was different than the river channels that they were used to traveling in. It was more like an underwater elevator, as soon as the kids entered they didn't have to swim anymore, they were just pushed calmly but quickly to their destination.

CHAPTER 13
GOOD-BYES

They climbed out of the pool onto Kevin's island in the grassy swamp of Never, Never Land. The dragonflies that had been protecting the fairy stones on the first day of summer had flown over the island. Chippy and Dougal were waiting at the edge of the pool. The summer was coming to an end, the first summer as water sprites.

"It's hard to believe that our summer started here and now it's ending here," Jake said, actually looking like he forgot for a minute about being mad at Grace. He was smiling, thinking back to the fairy hunt that first day of summer when they found their stones and a golf ball right here on this island.

"Yeah, this sucks, summer ending," Cole hung his head, but quickly looked up with a smile. "But we still have time to try to make it across that hanging log thingy at the church camp ropes course."

"Why, I thought you'd never ask," Jake drawled, pretending to consult a pocket watch. "Yes indeedy, sir, I believe we do have time." He cleared his throat, and added, "I mean, yeah, dude, you're on!"

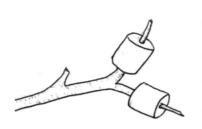

Julia giggled as Chippy jumped into her arms to greet her. "And we definitely have time to play King of the Dock, and Tag around the Dock, and Steal the Bacon, and have a scavenger hunt and maybe even a talent show or play Sardines. And tonight we have to have s'mores and play Flashlight Tag too," she announced, fiddling with Chippy's hair.

"Well no point standing around talking about it, show me this log," Harvey said. "I'm a Boy Scout you know. Log walking is nothing."

"Follow me!" Cole raised up his arm and began marching off across the swamp's log bridge and into the dense woods heading back toward camp. Jake marched on after him and Harvey followed. Dougal joined the line, marching with the boys.

Grace laughed at the silly puppy. She turned to Olivia, "Let's go call your parents and see if you can stay all day. My parents can bring you guys home tonight."

"Yes, yes, you definitely have to," Julia urged, taking Olivia's hand. The three girls ran together through the woods, planning their afternoon and evening of camp fun.

*****

The camp kids had all learned and seen so much. They would spend the winter using their stones when they could, and checking up with one another on their Sees All. They would dream of collecting golf balls and buying more things at the water sprite stores, of seeing Serpy and mermaids and ocean animals. They would listen more carefully to the news and pay more attention to their geography and history lessons in social studies class.

And they would wonder if the magic of their stones would disappear in three years like Mr. Snyder said. That would mean that they would at least get one more summer, hopefully two. But most of all they would think about camp and their camp friends, counting down the days until they would return for more sprite adventures.

Coming Soon

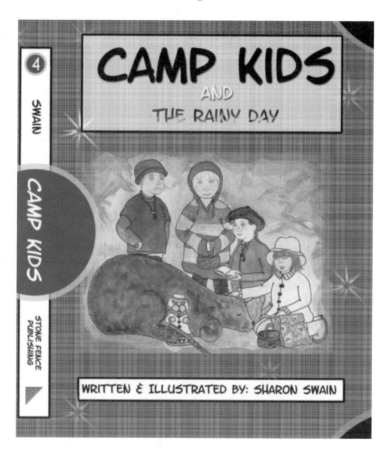

www.campkidsbooks.com